Fix it!

illustrated by Georgie Birkett

Child's Play (International) Ltd
Swindon Auburn ME Sydney

ISBN 978-1-84643-286-6

Printed in China
1 3 5 7 9 10 8 6 4 2
www.childs-play.com

Oh dear! Are all these toys broken?

Oh no! Look at my teddy. Can you fix it?

All charged up. Will my robot work now?

Wheel repair! I'll use my screwdriver.

Should I stick this lid with the tape?

There we are, as good as new!

They're all fixed. Where can I put them?

Let's build a toy box. Can I help?

Do you think we've forgotten anything?

We need more paint. I'd like this one.

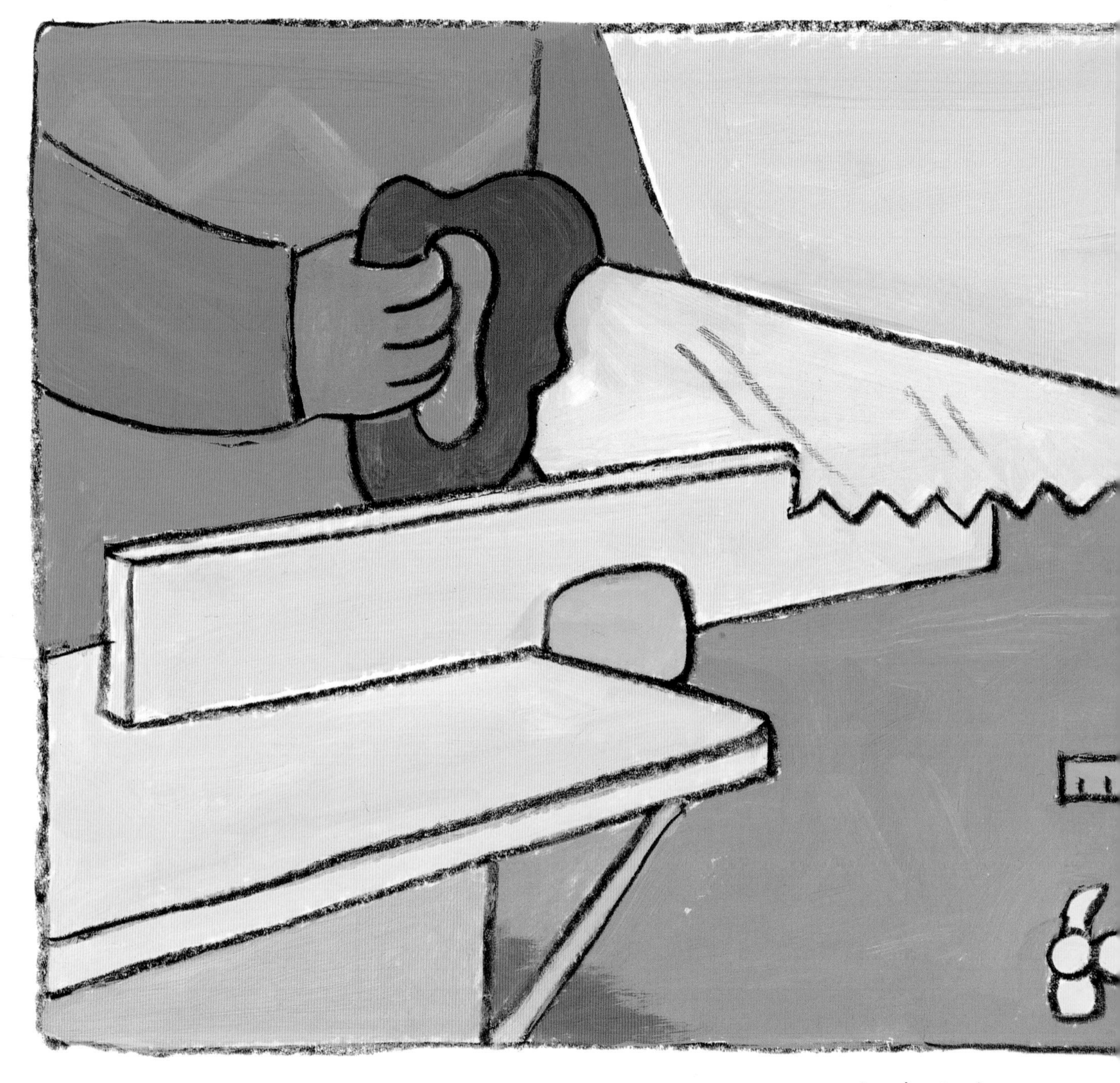

We need to cut the wood to the right length

Should I cut this piece with my saw?

I'll measure this. Is it one of the sides?

We need two of each. Do they match?

My head hurts! Why is the drill so noisy?

My drill is much better. It's very quiet!

How many nails do we need? Be careful!

I don't want to hit my fingers.

Let's put this on. Is it one of your old shirts?

This roller makes it easy to paint.

Are there any other shapes to paint?

How long will the paint take to dry?

A new toy box for all my toys. Great job!